D0432059

HOWARD ARTHUR

MAG

TEDDY THOMPSON

KENT DRYDEN

Diesen, Deborah.
Picture day perfection /
2013
3330 243 5107
gi 0 /1
W

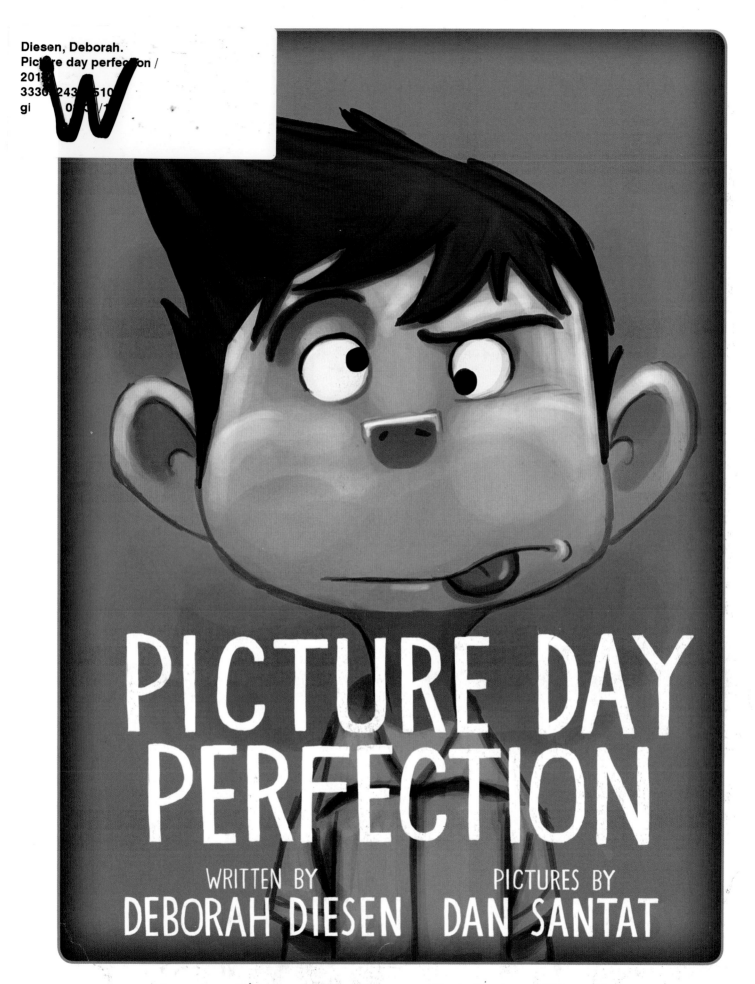

PICTURE DAY PERFECTION

WRITTEN BY
DEBORAH DIESEN

PICTURES BY
DAN SANTAT

Abrams Books for Young Readers, New York

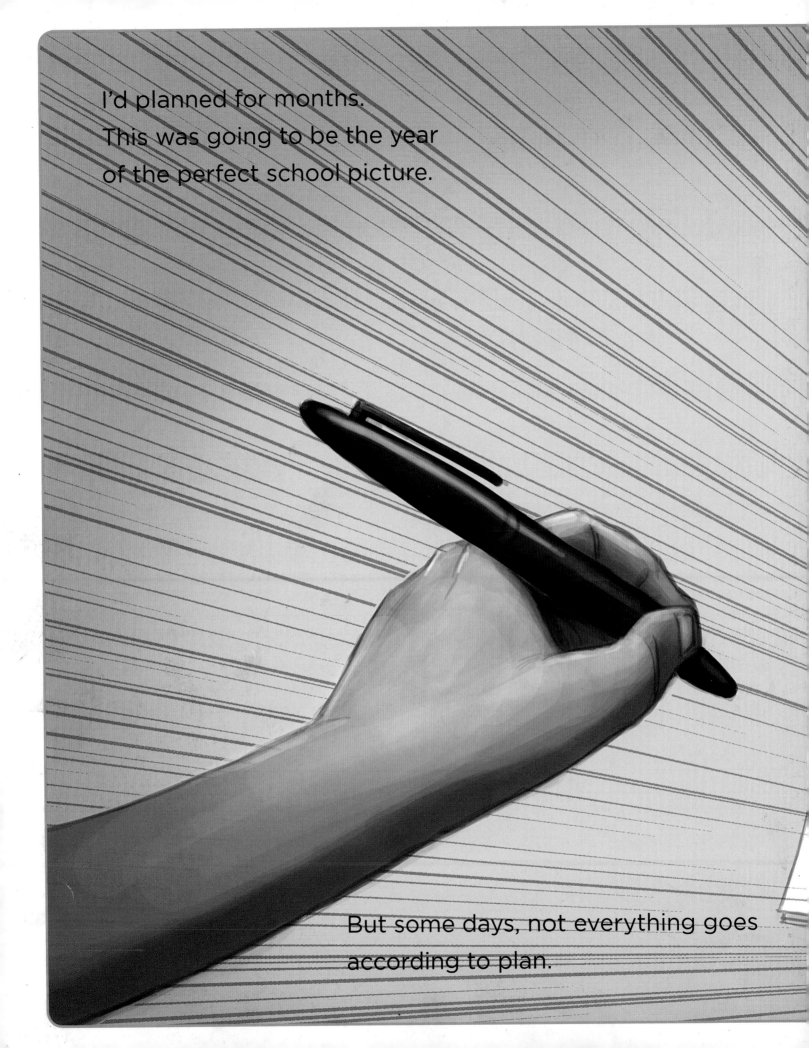

I'd planned for months.
This was going to be the year
of the perfect school picture.

But some days, not everything goes
according to plan.

The day started with the worst case of bedhead *ever*.

EXHIBIT A: FRONT VIEW

EXHIBIT C: BACK VIEW

EXHIBIT B: SIDE VIEW

EXHIBIT D: THE LOOK ON MY BROTHER'S FACE WHEN HE SAW MY HAIR.

Then it took me *quite* some time to unearth my favorite shirt. I finally found it at the *very* bottom of the hamper.

You might call it "stained."
You might call it "wrinkled."
You might even call it "smelly."
You wouldn't be wrong.

Breakfast was "Picture Day Pancakes," a family tradition. This year's festivities involved a small syrup disaster.

More accurately described as a *large* syrup disaster.
And it occurred exactly as the bus pulled up.

I had a feeling we'd be getting a new family tradition.

On the bus, I got into a small bit of trouble.

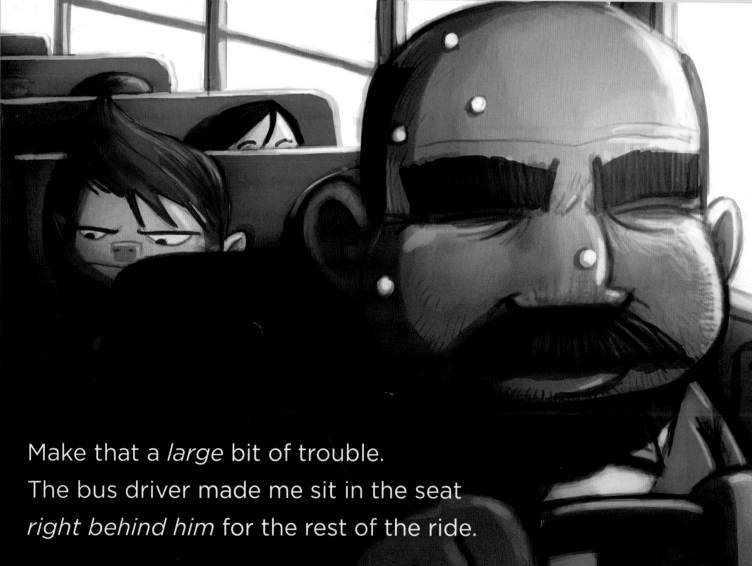

Make that a *large* bit of trouble.
The bus driver made me sit in the seat
right behind him for the rest of the ride.

By the time I got into school, my picture day face was fixed in a *scowl*.

In class, Mrs. Smith collected our photo order forms. Do you think my mom checked "Emerald Green" for my photo background? Or "Peacock Blue"? Or "Pizzazzy Purple"? No. Once again, of all the backgrounds in the world, Mom checked snoring-boring "Traditional Gray."

No one gets "Traditional Gray."

Except for me.

And it just so happens to be the only color in the
world that makes my favorite shirt disappear.
All but the stains and the wrinkles.

After that, the teacher had us all stand up and practice our Picture Day smiles. Personally, I thought we needed a little something to get us in the Picture Day mood.

Whoops!
Got myself in trouble.

Again.

Luckily, I got to rejoin the class in time for Art.
Art involved quite a lot of paint.

Or at least it did for *me*.

Finally, it was time to line up for our photos.

Ned, just in front of me, got the *last* complimentary plastic comb.

I watched as classmate after classmate smiled for the camera. I got queasy listening to everyone say "Cheese."

I can't *stand* cheese.

The mere thought of it turns me green! *Deeply* green. And just as my face reached its most *awful* pea-green shade, it was . . . *my turn.*

I stepped forward.

I sat down on the stool.

It was hard as a rock, and cold as an iceberg.

"Just a sec," said the photographer as he fiddled with the camera knobs.

As I sat and waited, everything
that had happened rushed through
my mind. The monstrous messes.
The muddles and the mix-ups. The
whole day, from the moment I'd
rolled out of bed, had gone . . .

Even better than planned!
This year, I was finally going to
have *the perfect school picture.*

And that's when I heard a

CLICK

In a flash, all my hard work—

my perfectly tangled hair,
my perfectly rumpled shirt,
my perfectly sticky face,
my perfectly composed scowl,
that perfect boring background,
those perfect paint splatters,
that perfect sickly pallor—

WASTED!
USELESS!
RUINED,

in a moment of weakness,
by an unexpected smile.

Mom says it's my best picture ever.

But just *wait* till she sees *next* year's.

17

18

24

PICTURE DAY

25

31

For my siblings, Tom and Ann
        -D.D.

For Alek and Kyle
        -D.S.

THE ILLUSTRATIONS IN THIS BOOK
WERE MADE IN ADOBE PHOTOSHOP.

Cataloging-in-Publication Data has been
applied for and may be obtained from the
Library of Congress.
ISBN: 978-1-4197-0844-2

Text copyright © 2013 Deborah Diesen
Illustrations copyright © 2013 Dan Santat

Book design by Chad W. Beckerman

Published in 2013 by Abrams Books for Young
Readers, an imprint of Abrams. All rights
reserved. No portion of this book may be
reproduced, stored in a retrieval system,
or transmitted in any form or by any means,
mechanical, electronic, photocopying,
recording, or otherwise, without written
permission from the publisher.

Printed and bound in China
10 9 8 7 6

Abrams Books for Young Readers are
available at special discounts when
purchased in quantity for premiums and
promotions as well as fundraising or
educational use. Special editions can also
be created to specification. For details,
contact specialsales@abramsbooks.com
or the address below.

 ABRAMS The Art of Books
195 Broadway, New York, NY 10007
abramsbooks.com

MICHAEL ELLIOT

JEFF JEFFERSON

HANK CHOI

KARINA STEVENS